© 2023 Jasdomin Santana

First Edition

ISBN: 979-8-9890864-7-4

This book is self-published by Jasdomin Santana
Contact: jasdomin@outlook.com
Illustrations by Isa Saldanha

This is a work of fiction. Names, characters, businesses, places, events, locales, and incidents are either the products of the author's imagination or used in a fictitious manner. Any resemblance to actual persons, living or dead, or actual events is purely coincidental.

Printed in the United States of America

Jasdomin Santana

Gameress
꞊SQUAD꞊
ᐯiDEO GAMES and ᐯALOR

Illustrated by Isa Saldanha

Meet Atheni, leader so grand,
With her shield, Ooni, and a hero band.
A gemstone bright gives her power and might,
Together they shine, a dazzling sight!

Mysti splashes with water's embrace,
Rubi whispers to creatures, a gentle face.
Nari's tricks turn foes into friends,
Sophi's monsters, on elements, they depend.

Roxi molds earth, Mercuri's strong,
Astroidi's strategies never go wrong.
Medi heals, Genevi's immortal and wise,
Sunni fights, Aivi's gadgets surprise!

GAMING CLUB

"Superlox!" they cheered, a game to explore,
With gemstone powers, never a bore.

"Into Superlox,
with a joyous sound,
With friends they played,
adventures they found.

A troll appeared with
messages mean,
Atheni said, "Stay positive,
don't be unseen."

The troll was rude; Rubi calmed the way,
"We'll face this together," Atheni did say

A team meeting called, with
wisdom they spoke,
"We'll understand this troll,"
no kindness was broke.

Through rivers and paths,
they searched with a glow,

Each hero's power in a wonderful flow.

WORLDS EXPLORER

The troll's lair found, with courage, they stood,
Nari was ready, their mission understood.

"Approach with kindness," Atheni declared,
Her gemstone shined, their hearts were prepared.

A battle began, but no hurt was their aim,

They used their powers in understanding's name

The troll paused, confused by their grace,
"Why are you so kind?" he asked, a puzzled face.

"To understand,"
Atheni replied,
The troll's tears fell,
his meanness had died

"You can change,"
Rubi warmly said,
"Be our friend,"
Atheni's hand she led.

"I will change,"
the troll replied,
"With friends like you,"
he no longer lied.

A celebration, a victory sweet,
A friend was made, bullying was beat.

Back at school,
they remembered the day,
"Kindness wins," was all they'd say.

Superlox was joyous, troll now a friend,
Atheni, Ooni, heroes till the end.

In games or life,
Atheni's wisdom did call,

"Be kind, be brave, love
conquers all."

Made in the USA
Middletown, DE
03 January 2024